LEMONY Snicket

13 Words

MAIRA KALMAN

HARPER

An Imprint of HarperCollinsPublishers

WORD NUMBER 1:
Bird

The bird sits
on the table.

WORD NUMBER 2:
DESPONDENT

The bird
is despondent.

MUSHY PEAS
OOOOO

KAFKA

In fact, she is so sad that
she hops off the table to look
for something to cheer her up.

WORD NUMBER 3:
CAKE

Under the table is a cake.

It is in a box tied up with string.
The bird unties the string and opens the box
to see what kind of cake is inside.

There are all kinds of cakes around town.
There is vanilla cake with chocolate icing and candles.

There is chocolate cake with vanilla icing and
no candles but very pretty flowers all around.

There is lemon cake with
a picture of a lemon on the top.

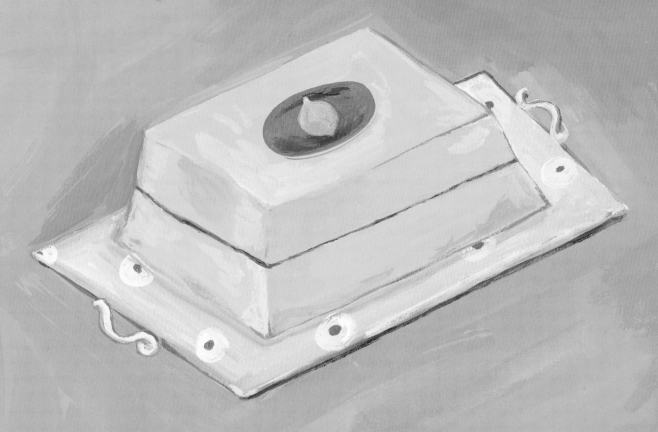

There is poppy seed cake with little
poppy seeds everywhere, making a mess.

WORD NUMBER 4:

Dog

The cake in the box is
strawberry shortcake.

"Hey, that'll cheer you up,"
says the dog.
"How about we eat it together?"
They sit at the table and
share the cake.

WORD NUMBER 5: BUSY

The bird and the dog have finished eating the cake.
They have even licked all of the icing off the box.
They have stacked up their dishes in the sink.

"That hit the spot," says the dog,
"but now I think you'd better get busy."

"It's time for you to paint those ladders, Bird.

Eleven ladders in ten colors.

That's a busy afternoon.
I'll go out for a while so you can keep your mind on painting."

WORD NUMBER 6:
ConvertiBLE

Outside is a glamorous green convertible
ready to take the dog into town.

WORD NUMBER 7: Goat

The driver of the convertible is a goat.
He is wearing a spiffy jacket.

They drive down a twisty two-lane highway.

"So where are we going?" asks the goat.

"Well, the bird is busy painting ladders,"
says the dog, "but she seems a little
sad, even after she ate some cake.
I'd like to go find something
that might cheer her up."

WORD NUMBER 8: Hat

"Do you know what's great?" says the goat.
"A hat. Nothing cheers folks up like a hat."
"That's a swell idea," says the dog.
"Let's go someplace where we can buy a hat."

Back at home,
the bird is busy,
but still despondent.

WORD NUMBER 9:
HABERDASHERY

The goat stops the convertible right in front of the haberdashery. A haberdashery is a store where you might find a good hat.

"This is the place, Dog," says the goat.

WORD NUMBER 10:

SCARLEt

The door of the haberdashery
is painted scarlet.

WORD NUMBER 11:

BABY

The owner of the haberdashery is a baby.

"Good afternoon," the baby says. "How have you been lately?"

"Fine, thanks. First I had some cake.

Now my friend is busy painting eleven ladders in ten colors.

The bird, who is the friend I was talking about, seems a little despondent, so I came here to the haberdashery to buy her a hat."

"Swell," says the baby.

The dog takes a long time with the hats.
Look at them all!

WORD NUMBER 12: PANACHE

The dog has finally chosen one hat for himself and one for the bird. "Both those hats have tons of panache," says the baby, putting them in boxes.

"What does that mean, 'feathers'?" asks the dog.

"Not just feathers," the baby says. "A sense of style and excitement, a kind of verve or swagger. You know what I mean?"

"Yes," says the dog. The goat honks the horn of the convertible.

The dog and the goat drive back home
in the convertible in a state of great excitement.

"Ta-da!" says the dog when he gets home, plunking down the two boxes on the table. "Look what I got you, my fine feathered friend!" Inside the boxes are the hats with panache, of course.

WORD NUMBER 13: MEZZO-SOPRANO

The bird likes her hat very much.

The dog likes his, too.

It's about five thirty when a mezzo-soprano walks through the door carrying a box with another cake inside.
"Whew," she says.
"I just spent all afternoon singing arias on a stage.
I need to put my feet up and have some cake.
How was your day?"

The dog tells the mezzo-soprano everything that has happened, and the mezzo-soprano decides to sing about it.

There once was a BiRd and there once was a DOg,

And the bird was DESPONdENT, or sad,

A pensive frown on her BUSY beak,

No matter that CAKE could be had.

The GOAt suggested a CONVERTiBLE drive,

To purchase a cheering-up Hat,

At a HABERdASHERY with a SCARLEt door,

And a BABY to sell them just that.

The hats have PANACHE, of course, of course,

A sense of excitement and style,

The MEZZO-SOPRANO is done with her song,

So let's all just eat for a while.

Tra la, tra la, tra la, tra la,

And sing those tra las once more.

Tra la, tra la, tra la, tra la,

Try not to get crumbs on the floor.

It is a beautiful song.
It has been a good day.

Everyone, everyone,
everyone, everyone
has cake.

Although the bird,
to tell you the truth,
is still a little despondent.